D1343946

500 651 761 8F

TALES OF WONDER

AND MAGIC

COLLECTED BY

BERLIE DOHERTY

ILLUSTRATED BY

JUAN WIJNGAARD

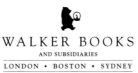

WALKER BOOKS

AND SUBSIDIARIES

LONDON · BOSTON · SYDNEY

CONTENTS

INTRODUCTION

A magic story is about something that we wish could really happen. I think it's also a story that casts a spell on the reader, so they can't get it out of their minds or their dreams. In every one of these stories we find something marvellous or strange happening, a power or mystery that can't be explained but can only be wondered at. I think that's the real essence of the magical tale.

Most of the tales in this collection come from very ancient sources and will have been told or retold for hundreds of years, like *Tamlane*, *The Black Bull of Norroway* and *The Girl from Llyn Y Fan Fach*, from Scotland, Ireland and Wales. They are still very powerful today and all are beautifully told.

My favourite story is the haunting Shetland tale, *The Woman of the Sea*. That is the sort that stays in your heart for ever, and affects people so much that they tell it in many different ways, as if it had become part of their own experience.

For the slaves in *The People Could Fly* the only escape from their unbearable lives is by magic. The power of the story lies in the reader's wish that it could be true. It sounds true, because of the way it's told, as though somebody is actually remembering seeing such a thing, and that is another secret of a good magical tale.

The Aboriginal story of *Mirragen the Cat-man* sets magic against cunning in the pursuit of a monster, and the same kind of battle is fought to free the moon in the lyrical story of *The Bogles and the Moon*.

In several of the stories we hear about different worlds, often under the sea or in a lake, and in the African story of *Chura and Marwe* we actually go there. In this story, as in many of the others, love is the most powerful magic of all, and can make anything possible.

I was asked to add a story of my own to the collection and, though *The Girl Who Couldn't Walk* is one that I made up, I've written it in the style of folk-magic. Like the tribal Canadian story *The Boy of the Red Twilight Sky*, it's about a deep longing. You can't really understand what happens in these stories; you just have to believe it might, just as you believe dreams.

Above everything else, I chose these particular stories because I love the way they are told. I always want to find magic in the language of stories. I like the words to sing like the words of songs, and the stories to linger in my head like music. That's what makes them unforgettable.

The Girl from Llyn Y Fan Fach

In the heart of the mountains in the old county of Carmarthenshire lies a lonely lake called Llyn y Fan Fach. Close by, in Blaensawdde Farm, a boy lived with his widowed mother. His father had died years before, and the boy and his mother kept the farm going as best they could.

One fine afternoon in early August when the boy was watching his cattle on the shore of the lake he saw the face of a girl in the water. He looked over his shoulder to see the girl whose face was mirrored there, but there was no one to be seen, and when he turned back to the lake he saw only the sun glinting on the water and the breeze stirring the rushes. He thought about it all the way home. He was sure he had not been dreaming.

Next day, once again he drove his cattle from Blaensawdde to the lake shore. It was a fine day and sunlight danced on the surface. He stared into the water hoping to see the girl's face, but this time nothing disturbed its smooth surface.

He turned his head for a while to watch his cows, and when he looked at the lake again, there she was, sitting among the rushes, combing her hair with a comb that flashed gold in the sun.

She was the most beautiful girl he had ever seen. He held out his hand to her, hoping she would come closer, but she stayed among the rushes, combing her long hair. He remembered the bread and cheese his mother had given him that morning, and he took it from his pocket, stretched out his hand and offered it to the girl.

She moved closer to look at the bread he offered her, then smiled and said, "Your bread's too hard. You can't catch me."

Then she vanished leaving scarcely a ripple, and though he waited for a long time he did not see her again. The sun set behind the mountain and the boy made his way thoughtfully home, driving his cattle before him in the dusk.

That night he told his mother about the girl he had seen in the lake, and when he came to the part where the girl said, "Your bread's too hard. You can't catch me," his mother nodded her head.

10

"Tomorrow," she said, "I'll give you some uncooked dough. Perhaps she'd like that better."

Next morning the boy returned to the lakeside with the cows, and sat a long time beside the calm water hoping to see her. Hours passed but the girl did not come. Not a sound was to be heard except the distant lowing of a cow on the mountain track, and the soft lapping of lake water on the shingle.

The afternoon had almost gone and the sun had moved towards the west when the waters of the lake began to boil, and he saw her again quite close to him. The boy walked to the water's edge, offering the dough his mother had given him. Her smile teased him and she said, "Your bread's too soggy. You can't catch me."

In a moment she had disappeared into the depths of the lake.

That night, when the boy told his mother the story, she decided to bake another loaf, this time lightly, not too crisp and not too moist.

The following day a light rain was falling on the lake, and the mountains were shawled in mist as though someone had drawn a thick blanket over the surface of the lake during the night. In the heart of such a vast silence the boy felt lonely and sad. He felt little hope of seeing the girl that day. But still he kept an eye on the lake. Its water was dark and full of mystery.

Then during the afternoon the mist rose, the rain stopped, the sun appeared, and the surface of the water

began to boil like molten silver. He saw her almost at once, a shaft of sunlight shining on her face and hair. He walked straight through the water towards her until she was so close that he could hold out his slice of bread to her. She took it from his hand, tasted and ate it.

Suddenly the boy fought away his shyness and asked her to marry him. The girl from the lake thought a while about his question, and at last she smiled and said, "I will marry you and be your faithful wife until you strike me three times without reason."

The boy laughed with delight because he knew he loved her too much to strike her, with or without a reason. He took her hand in his, and she smiled.

Then, as suddenly as ever, she vanished into the lake. Was she only teasing him? He waited for a while, perplexed. Then he saw not one beautiful girl but two, as alike as peas in a pod, rising out of the water together and with them came an old man with silver hair.

"You may marry my daughter," said the old man, "if you can tell which one of them is your true love."

12

The young man looked carefully at the two beautiful women. They were identical. They had the same hair, the same eyes, the same height, the same little smile. There was nothing to choose between them.

He looked for a long time, worried that if he picked the wrong girl their father would not let him marry either of them. He looked down at their hands. Was there a difference between them? There was none. Then he stared at their feet and as he did so he saw one of the girls move her right foot slightly.

He looked at her, and knew for certain that she was his true love, and that she had moved her foot as a signal to help him to choose her. He walked towards her through the water and took her hand in his.

"You have chosen right," said the old man. "Be a faithful husband to her, and remember, if you strike her three times without cause she must leave you and return to the lake. And now, for her wedding dowry she can have as many sheep, cattle and horses as she can count while holding her breath."

The girl breathed in deeply and began to count: "One, two, three, four, five! One, two, three, four, five! One, two, three, four, five!" until she had to gulp for air.

The young man could hardly believe his eyes. Flocks of sheep and herds of cattle and horses, a procession of fine, healthy animals one by one broke the surface of the water and waded ashore, shook the waters from their coats and began to graze at the lakeside.

After the wedding the young couple went to live at a farm called Esgair Llaethdy, a few miles from the village of Myddfai and not very far from Llyn y Fan Fach. There they lived together in great happiness.

The young man soon realized he had chosen a good wife. She was loving and hard working, kept the house clean and helped him on the farm. As the years went by they grew prosperous and three sons were born to them. No family could have been happier than the family at Esgair Llaethdy.

One day they had to go to a funeral because a neighbour had died. The church was full of sorrow and tears, but the beautiful woman from Llyn y Fan Fach began to laugh aloud. The congregation stared at her, and her embarrassed husband struck her lightly on the shoulder and whispered to her to be quiet.

"I was happy," she said later, "because our neighbour has gone to a better place and his suffering

14

is over. But now I feel sad because you have struck me without good cause. If you do it twice more you will lose me."

Her husband was sorry and vowed to be more careful in future.

One evening some time later, as he was coming home after working hard all day in the fields, he found a horseshoe on the ground. It was a bright, new shoe which he knew one of his horses had lost, and he picked it up, intending to shoe the horse next day.

His wife was in the kitchen but his supper wasn't ready yet. "Hey! What about my supper?" he asked, playfully tapping her shoulder with the horseshoe.

She turned quickly to him, her face pale.

"That's the second time you've struck me without cause," she said. "If you do it once more you will lose me."

He realized what he had done and made a vow that he would never let it happen again.

For a long time he was careful and they were happy, but one day the couple were invited to a christening. The farmer's wife was not looking forward to the prospect of a long walk.

"We can ride on horseback," said her husband.

So they went into the field to catch one of the horses. That day the horses were frisky and would not be caught. Every time they were approached they tossed their manes and galloped away.

At last the beautiful woman from Llyn y Fan Fach outran her husband and caught one of the horses by the mane. She called to her husband to throw the bridle quickly. He threw it with all his might, and instead of landing at her feet the bridle struck her leg. She let the horse go and stared at him, her flushed face suddenly as ghostly as the face of a stranger. She turned and ran from him like a wild pony, calling the animals as she fled:

Come Brindle-back, come Speckle-face,
Come Red-flank, come old White-face,
Come White Bull from the prince's court,
Come little black calf,
Come four blue bullocks from the meadow.
Come home, come all, come home.

The cattle left their grazing and followed her, milking cows and heifers and calves, the four bullocks and the old white bull, all galloped with thundering hooves after her, and the horses stopped frisking and followed her call as she ran over the fields towards Llyn y Fan Fach.

There they all splashed through the water into the depths to disappear below the surface of the lake.

He could not believe she had gone. He climbed the mountain track to the lake time after time, and sat grieving on the shore, watching the water for his beautiful, beloved wife.

Sometimes, on summer afternoons when the sun turned the surface of the water to quicksilver, he would fancy he saw her face in the waters of Llyn y Fan Fach. But she never returned to keep him company on the lonely shore of the lake that lies to this day hidden like a secret in its circle of dark mountains.

CHURA AND MARWE

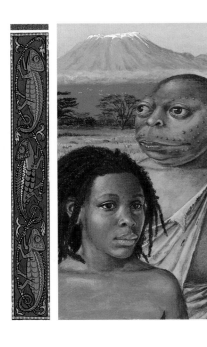

Far to the east of the world there is a great mountain, higher even than this one, for the top is lacquered with silver every month of the year. Upon the slopes of this mountain there once lived a boy and a girl. He was called Chura and she Marwe and they were slave children, got cheap and kept by a household of the Chagga people to watch crops and herd goats.

Now Chura had a face like a toad's and Marwe was so beautiful that when people saw them together they exclaimed, "Eh! How is it that God could make two so different?"

That, however, was not how Marwe saw it. Chura was her companion and the only one she had. They loved each other dearly, were happy together and only when they were together, for they had little else to be happy about.

One day they were sent to watch a field and keep the monkeys from eating the beans. The place was on the lower slopes of the mountain, a clearing in the forest, and there all day the children sat beating a pot with a stick whenever they heard a monkey chatter thievishly behind the wall of leaves.

Hemmed in with tall trees, the field was airless and hot and by late afternoon they could stand their thirst no longer. They slipped off to where a stream, cold from the snows above, fell noisily down a cliff into a pool. The water there was deep and upon its dark surface one leaf floated in a circle all day. Here they drank hastily, washed the tiredness from their faces, then ran back to the field. Alas, in the time they had been away the monkeys had stripped it.

Marwe wept and Chura stared at the plundered bean plants with a bleak face. The folk they worked for were harsh and the children knew they would be beaten. Chura tried to comfort his friend but there was little of that he could give her and at last, in despair, she ran into the forest. Chura followed, calling for her to stop, and was just in time to see her throw herself into the pool where, at once, she sank from sight.

Chura could not swim and he knew the pool to be deep. He ran round the edge calling, but it was no

20

use. The dark water quietened, the leaf again circled placidly and Marwe was gone.

Chura went back to the household and told those who owned him of the loss of Marwe and the crop. They followed him to the pool, where nothing was to be seen, and then to the field, where the sight of ruined plants made them angry. They beat Chura and some days later, grieving for Marwe and tired of ill treatment, he ran away and the Chagga never saw him again.

Soon another pair of children watched the crops or herded goats, and whether they found life better than Chura and Marwe had is unknown.

⊠ ⊠ ⊠

When Marwe flung herself into the pool she sank slowly through water which changed from the bright light of noon to the deep blue of late evening and finally to the darkness of a night with neither moon nor stars. And there she stepped out into the Underworld, shook water from her hair and wandered, chilled to the heart by the greyness of the place.

Presently she came to a hut on the slope of a hill with an old woman outside preparing supper for the small children playing on the swept earth at her feet. Beyond the hut, just where the hill curved over and away, was a village that seemed as if it had just been built, for the logs of the stockade were white as if the bark had been stripped from them that day and the thatch of the houses was new-dried and trim.

The old woman asked Marwe where she was going, and Marwe replied timidly that she was a stranger and alone and wanted to go to the village she saw above to ask for food and perhaps work so that she could live her life.

"It's not yet time to go there," said the woman. "Stay with me and work here. You'll not go hungry or lack a place by the fire if you do so."

So Marwe accepted this offer and lived with the old woman. She cared for the children, fetched water from the stream and weeded a garden. Her new mistress was kind and so life for Marwe went on without hardship. Only sometimes she pined for the sunlight and bird song of the world above, for here it was never anything but grey. And always she longed for Chura.

And now let us follow what happened to him.

He drifted from village to village of the Chagga asking for food and work but, because of his ugliness, no one would take him in. Food they offered hastily and then they told him uneasily to go. It seemed to

22

men and even more to women that such an ill-favoured face must have been earned by great evil and could only bring with it worse luck.

So, wandering from hamlet to village, gradually inching his way round the mountain, he was fed by unwilling charity or, more often, by what small game he could kill or field he could rob. As the years passed he grew strong and hard but no better looking.

One day he left the forest and the tall grass of the foothills and walked north into the sun-bitten plain. Here the trees were bleached and shrunken, standing wide apart, their thin leaves throwing little shade. Between them the ants built red towers and covered every dead leaf or stick with a crust of dry earth. A juiceless land where grass was scarce and water more so, and here lived the Masai.

They are a people who greatly love three things: children, cattle and war. Standing like storks upon one leg, holding spears with blades long as an arm, and shields blazing with colour, they guarded their cattle and looked with amused indifference upon the lives of other men.

They found Chura wandering and thirsty, carelessly decided not to kill him, made him a servant. At his ugliness they only laughed.

"What's it to us if you look like a toad," they shouted. "All men other than Masai are animals any-way. And usually look like them."

So Chura milked cows, mended cattle fences and made himself useful until one night a lion attacked the calves. Then he took a spear from a hut and went out and killed it.

"Wah!" said the Masai when they came running and found Chura with the great beast dead at his feet. "Alone and without a shield! This is a new light you show yourself in. Well, you weren't born Masai, though plainly some mistake's been made by Asis over that. Somewhere within you there must be a Masai of sorts, otherwise you couldn't have done this. We'll accept you for one."

So they gave him the spear he had borrowed, and a shield whose weight made him stagger. When the lion's skin had been cured they made from it a head-dress that framed Chura's face in a circle of tawny hair and added two feet to his height.

"There, now you look almost human," they said. "Only something must be done about that name of yours. It means toad and no Masai could live with it."

"Well then, what am I to be called?" asked Chura.

"Hmm. Punda Malia (Donkey)?" suggested one.

"No, no, Kifaru (Rhino)," said another.

"What about Nguruwe (Pig)?" threw in another.

"If you can't be civil..." began Chura, taking a firm grip on his spear.

"Heh! Keep your temper, Brother. We mean no harm. Now, what can your name be...?"

They called for a pot of beer and spent a happy evening making suggestions and falling about with laughter at their own wit. But finally they pulled themselves together and found for Chura a name which seemed to them far more suitable than the one he had brought with him.

⊠　⊠　⊠

When Marwe had lived for a number of years in the Underworld and grown to be as beautiful a woman as she had been a child, she became homesick. The old woman noticed her sadness and asked what caused it. Marwe hesitated, because she did not want to seem ungrateful for the kindness that had been given to her but, in the end, she said that she pined to go back to her own world.

The old woman was not offended. "Ah," she said, "then it's time you went to the village. In this matter I can't help but they may."

Next day Marwe climbed the hill and waited at the village gate. When she had sat there for some time a number of old men came out. They were dressed in cotton robes that shone through the gloom about and they greeted her and asked what she wanted. Marwe replied that she wished to return to the world above.

"Hmm," they said. "We'll see, yes, we'll see."

Then one who seemed the most important among them asked, "Child, which would you sooner have, the warm or the cold?"

The question bewildered Marwe. "I don't understand," she replied.

Shadows seemed to cross their faces and their voices grew fainter. "That's nothing to us," they said. "You've heard our question and we can do nothing unless you answer. Which would you prefer, the warm or the cold?"

Marwe understood that this was a test which it must be important for her to consider with care.

"Warmth ... or cold?" she pondered. "Well, everyone would sooner have warmth than cold because cold is bitter and difficult to endure, while warmth is life itself. Yet surely their riddle can't be as easy as that."

When she had thought again, as deeply as she could, it seemed that if the choice was between what is usually thought to be good and bad, her life pointed the other way.

"For," said she, "Chura was ugly and unwanted, yet he was kind and I loved him. And the Underworld is feared by everyone yet here I've met greater kindness than I ever knew in the sunlit world above."

And she made up her mind and said, "No matter what others believe, I'll trust my own wisdom and choose the cold."

The old men listened to her answer with faces from which she could read nothing and they offered her two pots. From the mouth of one rose steam while the other sent out a chill that stuck to the bone of a hand brought near it.

"Choose as you've chosen," they urged her, and so, faithful to her own belief, she dipped a hand into the cold pot and brought it out covered to the elbow with richly made bracelets.

"Don't hesitate to take more," they urged her. "Neither we nor the pots will be offended."

So she reached in her other arm and in turn both her feet and they came out heavy with bangles and anklets, heavy precious things made from copper and gold, ornaments worth more than the tribute of a whole tribe.

The old men smiled and told her she had chosen well and been wise. And still they loaded her with treasures, necklaces of shell, rings and ear-drops. They brought her a fine kilt worked all over with gold wire and beads that glowed blue as the skies she remembered from the world above.

"Now," they said, "we've one more gift: a piece of advice. When you are back in your own world you'll wish in time to marry and there'll be no shortage of those who'll ask for you. Go softly, don't hasten. Wait for someone with the name of Simba to ask, and choose him."

Then, gathering her robes clear of their feet, the old ones led her to the pool. Gently they urged her in and she rose like a thought until she broke the sunlit surface where the leaf still circled and birds sang in the trees about.

She left the water, sat upon the bank with the light

dancing on her finery, and waited for the world to find her. And very soon it did.

News spread that beside the pool in the forest sat a woman, rich and of amazing beauty, waiting for a husband. They flocked to her with offers – handsome young men, rich landowners, daring hunters, great warriors, even powerful chiefs. And all singing much the same tune: "Here's fame or wealth or power, or glory or beauty or ... if you'll marry *me*!"

She pointed at each one of them the same sharp little question, "What's your name?"

"Name! Why it's Nyati or Mamba or Tembo or Ndovu or..." and so on. No end of names and at all she shook her head and replied, "I'm sorry, but that will not be the name of my husband."

Now the news flew even as far as the plain, down where the cattle trudge through the dust, the lion hunts and the vulture sits upon the thorn. At last it reached Chura and at once he took spear and shield and came tirelessly running and his heart singing, "Marwe's back from the Underworld and I'll see her!"

When he came to where she sat beside her pool and cried "Marwe!" she recognized his ugliness even framed as it was by a lion's mane. Part of her laughed and the rest wept.

"Oh, Chura," she cried. "Why is life so unkind? I shall never love anyone but you yet my fate says that we can't marry."

"Then who can you marry?" he demanded.

"Only a man named Simba."

"But that's my name," he roared. "*Simba!* Lion! The Masai named me that when I killed a lion."

So, of course, they were married. What was there to stop them? It would have been striking fate across the face not to marry. But everyone marvelled that so beautiful a woman should choose so ugly a husband.

They paid no attention to them and – it's a strange thing and scarcely to be believed – but, do you know, the moment they were married something happened to his ugly toad's face and he became good to look at.

Well, passable.

So they say.

I don't imagine for one moment that Marwe cared either way.

The Bogles
and the Moon

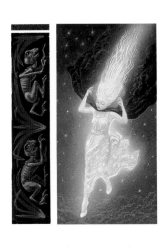

The moon was for ever hearing tales of what went on in swamp-country when her back was turned. In the end she decided to go down and see for herself. At the end of the month, leaving a single sliver of light in the sky, she wrapped herself in a black cloud-cloak, pulled the hood over her gleaming silver hair and slipped down to earth.

The place she chose was muddy and slippery. The path was bordered by clumps of reeds and grass, and on each side wide pools, dark and fathomless, rippled in the breeze. It was pitch dark. The only light was a shimmer from the moon's own silver shoes, a glow as faint as candle flame in the howling dark. As the moon picked her way along, dim night creatures – owls, bats and furry moths – fluttered past, and she could hear the Bogles' eerie wailing and see their will-o'-the-wisps dancing in the misty field. Every so often, when the moon's foot went too near the edge of the narrow path,

bony fingers reached quickly up from the water's depths: the Bogles were alert for prey.

At first, nothing could catch the moon. Her tread was as light as gossamer: she stepped nimbly, easily, from tussock to tussock; the Bogles snatched in vain. Then the moon's silver shoe slipped on a stone. She took hold of a handful of reeds to steady herself, and at once they coiled round her wrist and held her fast. More and more reeds snaked out of the darkness, till the moon was a prisoner, trapped and shivering.

All at once in the distance she heard the thin sound of a human voice, calling for help. A man was lost in the swamps, splashing past the pools and puddles, writhing clear of the Bogles' clutching hands, sobbing desperately for help. The moon knew that unless the man had light to find his path, he would soon be Bogles' meat. She shook the hood clear of her head, and let her silver hair stream down her back. In its sudden light the man saw firm land ahead of him, jumped thankfully on to the path and ran safely home. But the same silver light attracted Bogles from all the surrounding swamps.

Shielding their eyes against the light, they clustered round the moon and tied her even tighter, covering her with reeds and stones till every glimmer of her light was gone. Now there was no hope for creatures lost in the swamps at night. Without light, everything that passed was doomed. Cackling and whooping, the Bogles slithered back to their oozy dens to wait.

34

At first, the people who lived in the swamp village thought nothing was wrong. At the beginning of each new month, it was always dark; the moon always took days to show herself. But as the weeks passed, each night as dark as the last, the swamp Bogles grew hungrier and bolder. They took to prowling outside the windows of the houses, so that people had to bolt their doors, stay awake all night, and build roaring fires to keep the evil things at bay.

For two months this was how things were. The villagers were in despair. Then, one night, sitting with his cronies round the fire in the village inn, a farmer suddenly slapped his thigh and said, "Of course! That must have been the moon who saved me, that night when I was lost in the swamp. I saw a shining and I found my path; but I never thought till now that it was the moon. She's the Bogles' prisoner – and I know where she is."

Everyone ran for lanterns, pitchforks and scythes. A crowd surged down the village street, waving lights and jeering at the Bogles to show how brave they were. Then, at the edge of the village, they stopped so suddenly that those at the back fell cursing into those in front. The village wise woman, a toothless crone everyone took for a witch, was standing there, a guttering candle in one hand and a bony finger held up to her withered lips.

"Ssh!" she hissed. "You'll not scare Bogles with yells

and scythes. Cover your lanterns and feel your way through the swamp with sticks. Put a pebble under your tongue, each one of you, to stop you whispering and letting the Bogles know where you are."

They did as she said. A straggly line of men poked and picked its way along the paths between the swamp pools. Many of them were sure they were walking into Bogles' larders: they cast fearful eyes into the dark on either side, and muttered prayers for safety in their hearts.

At last they came to a pile of stinking, rotting weeds, and a heap of stones like the cairns men build to mark a grave. At once they did as the wise woman had advised. They threw open their cloaks and showed their lanterns all at once, and the sudden light sent the Bogles shrieking for cover. The men began prising up the stones and dragging away the reeds. Soon, from the ground below, there was the glitter of silver, and they saw the face of a woman more beautiful than any seen on earth before or since. The swamp pools for metres round were lit as bright as day; the moon's reed manacles slipped free of her wrists and she soared into the sky, like a dazzling beacon to light her rescuers home.

From that day to this the moon has kept a special watch on travellers in swamp land. But she takes care never to put herself in the Bogles' way again, and never ventures down to earth. She soars high out of reach in the sky, and her face is all earth dwellers ever see. 🦎

TAMLANE

A long time ago – so long ago that everyone now has forgotten exactly when – the Queen of the Faeries used to hold her court by night at Carterhaugh near Selkirk, where Ettrick Water sweeps round to join Yarrow Water before they both flow into the River Tweed.

Winter can be long and cruel in the high moors and lonely dales of the Borderland, and when the north wind skirled and shrieked through the leafless trees and blew the snow higher than walls and barns and cottages, the maidens of Ettrickdale and Yarrow, sitting in their bowers and sewing their silken seams, would drop their needlework and sigh for the spring when they could meet again on the pleasant plain of Carterhaugh.

Nowhere in all the brave Borderland, they thought, was there grass as green as the grass of Carterhaugh,

39

nowhere were the wild roses so delicate a pink, the bluebells so pure a colour, the broom such a blaze of gold; how pleasant it was, they thought, to meet there and gather flowers and play at ball and talk and laugh and dance and sing, remembering always to return to their homes before the sun set – because in the hours of darkness the plain belonged to the Little People.

Of all the maidens who played and talked and laughed and danced and sang on the green grass when the winter was past, the fairest and most courageous was the Lady Janet, whose parents loved her dearly and whose father had given her the land of Carterhaugh for her own.

One bright May morning she was playing with four and twenty other maidens; they were throwing high a coloured ball, laughing as they picked up their long silken dresses to run, barefoot, to catch it, when the Queen of the Faeries suddenly appeared in their midst.

"This is the last time you maidens may play here," she said in a cold, thin voice. "I forbid you to set foot again on the grass of Carterhaugh by day or by night, for now it belongs to young Tamlane." And she disappeared as suddenly as she had appeared.

Frightened, the maidens ran for their slippers and hastily pulled them on and braided up their hair, ready to obey the command of the Queen of the Faeries – all except the Lady Janet.

"What right has she to say that we cannot play here?"

40

fair Janet cried angrily. "This land is mine. My daddy gave it to me. The Little People are welcome to come here at night, but by day it is mine, and I shall come here whenever I want. And you'll all come and play here with me, won't you?"

But the four and twenty maidens shook their heads, because they were frightened of angering the Faery Queen, and they hurried back to their homes by the banks of the Yarrow and Ettrick Water, leaving fair Janet alone on the green plain, so that in the end she followed them with a sigh.

Yet when she got back to Bowhill, where she lived, she said nothing to her parents about the Queen of the Faeries.

When she awoke the next morning, she stretched her arms above her head, watched the first ray of the morning sun steal through the window, and wondered what she should do that day.

"I know," she thought. "I shall pick some flowers for my mammy, who loves me more than anything else in all the world. I shall pick her wild roses which are just tinged with pink, and the loveliest roses of all grow on the thorn bush by the well at Carterhaugh, which belongs to me."

Putting on her silken dress, which was as green as the grass on Carterhaugh, and her slippers, which were as red as the berries on the rowan tree, she combed out her long yellow hair and plaited it and wound the plait

42

round her head and fixed it in place with two golden combs on which sparkled emeralds, as green as her dress or the grass of Carterhaugh.

She gathered her long skirts in her hands and ran off to the meadow, to the thorn bush which grew by the well, and she had just picked the first white rosebud, so faintly tinged with pink, when an angry voice behind her cried, "Who are you? And what are you doing here at Carterhaugh?"

When Janet turned round, she saw before her a faery knight on a milk-white steed, which was shod with two shoes of silver and two of gold; the knight himself was dressed from head to foot in white, and on his dark, curling hair he wore a hat with a rose pink plume.

"Who are you? And what are you doing here at Carterhaugh?" the knight repeated.

"I am the Lady Janet," the maiden answered proudly. "And I am picking wild roses for my mammy because all this land belongs to me. My daddy gave it to me."

"I am Tamlane," the knight cried angrily, looking at Janet with eyes as cold and grey as the waters of Ettrick on a February day. "The Queen of the Faeries gave Carterhaugh to me, and you come here at your peril."

"From sunset to sunrise all this land is yours," fair Janet said. "Is that not enough for you?"

Slowly Tamlane shook his head and his milk-white steed whinnied and pawed the ground.

"Yesterday I played here with four and twenty maidens," Janet said, "and there was room enough for all of us and room to spare; today there should be room for you and me." And turning to the thorn bush, she continued picking the white rosebuds so faintly tinged with pink.

The anger faded from Tamlane's face and into his grey eyes came a strange, lost look.

"As you have come to gather wild roses for your mammy," he said, "today you may stay. But after this, Carterhaugh is mine and mine alone."

Without saying a word, fair Janet picked the last of the wild roses, and then she turned and stared up into the blue, blue sky, listening to the liquid trilling of the skylark which hovered overhead; and Tamlane turned his head and looked up with his sad grey eyes and sighed. "So long ago is it since last I heard the song of the lark on a May morning, that I had almost forgotten how beautiful it could be," he said, and tugging at the reins of his milk-white steed, he galloped off without another word, and Janet picked up the skirts of her silken dress in her left hand and walked slowly back to her home.

The next morning when she awoke she stretched her arms above her head and watched the first rays of the morning sun steal through the window, wondering what she should do that day.

"I know," she thought. "I shall pick some flowers for

my mammy, who loves me more than anything else in all the world. I shall pick her sprays of green broom afire with golden blossom, and the finest bush with the richest flowers grows not far from the well at Carterhaugh, which belongs to me."

Putting on her silken dress, which was as green as the grass on Carterhaugh, and her slippers, which were as red as the berries on the rowan tree, she combed out her long yellow hair, and plaited it, and wound the plait round her head, and fixed it in place with two golden combs on which sparkled emeralds, as green as her dress or the grass of Carterhaugh.

She gathered her long skirts in her hand and ran off to the meadow, to the broom which grew near the well. She had just broken off the first branch, when an angry voice behind her cried, "Who are you? And what are you doing here at Carterhaugh?"

When Janet turned round, she saw before her Tamlane on his milk-white steed, which was shod with two shoes of silver and two of gold; but this time the plume in his hat was gold like the blossom of the broom.

"I am the Lady Janet," the maiden answered quietly, "and I am picking golden broom for my mammy, because all this land belongs to me."

"It belongs to me!" Tamlane cried angrily, and his grey eyes were as cruel as Yarrow Water when the snows melt on the hills and the river thunders down in

45

search of victims among the weary sheep or the travellers who have lost their way.

"Yesterday I picked my mammy a bunch of wild roses and together we listened to the lark as it sang high up in the blue, blue sky," Janet said softly. "There was room enough for the two of us then, Tamlane, so why should there not be room today?" And turning to the bush, she continued picking the green branches with their golden blossom.

The anger faded from Tamlane's face and into his grey eyes there came again a strange, lost look.

"As you have come to gather broom for your mammy," he said, "today you may stay. But after this, Carterhaugh is mine and mine alone."

Without saying another word, fair Janet picked the last spray of golden broom, and then she sat down on the green grass and looked across the Yarrow to the distant moorlands and listened to the plaintive cry of the curlew; and Tamlane looked down at fair Janet with his sad grey eyes and sighed.

"So long is it since last I heard the song of the curlew on a May morning, that I had almost forgotten how beautiful it could be," he said, and he tugged at the reins of his milk-white steed and galloped off without another word, and Janet gathered the skirts of her silken dress in her right hand and walked slowly back to her home.

When fair Janet awoke the following morning, she made up her mind to gather for her mammy a bunch of wild hyacinths, and because the loveliest and bluest flowers grew by the well of Carterhaugh, she picked up her long green dress in one hand and ran off to the meadow.

When she reached the well, Tamlane was waiting for her on his milk-white steed, and the plume in his hat was blue like the bells of the wild hyacinth. This time, instead of challenging her, he watched in silence as she pulled the long-stemmed bluebells and then, when her bunch was complete, he dismounted and together they walked down to the banks of the Yarrow and sat there, listening to the melancholy cry of the peewit. And Tamlane looked at fair Janet and sighed. "So long is it since last I heard the cry of the peewit that I had almost forgotten how beautiful it could be," he said.

"Are there no birds in Faeryland," fair Janet asked, "that you sigh when you hear the song of the sky-lark and the sound of the curlew and the cry of the peewit?"

"The faeries have their own sweet music to dance to and have no need of the song of the birds," Tamlane answered. "But memory dies hard with me, for I am mortal born.

"My father was Randolph, Earl of Murray; my mother the sweetest lady in the land. But the Queen of the Faeries spied me when I was out hunting one day and wanted me to be her courtier. She sent a cold wind from the north that chilled me to the marrow and I fell from my horse and lay in a swoon on the ground.

"The Faery Queen had me carried to yonder green hill, where she tended me with magic herbs and many a strange charm. And now I am Tamlane, her favourite knight, and with each successive day my mortal memory fades like some dimly remembered dream."

"And are you not content to live in Faeryland, where everyone is happy and no one is ever ill?" fair Janet asked.

"Once I might have been content," Tamlane answered, "but now that I have met you, Janet, I wish with all my heart the spell could be lifted so that I might wed you."

"What the Queen of the Faeries can do, that I can undo," Janet said, "because I too shall not be content until you are a mortal man and wed me. Tell me what must be done and I will do it."

"The spell is powerful, and to break it you will need more courage than any other maiden in all the

Borderland. You must return to your home and go your way throughout the summer and the autumn, giving no thought to Tamlane, and avoiding by day and night the green plain of Carterhaugh.

"And then, on the last night of October, which is Hallowe'en, if you have courage enough to try to break the spell, fair Janet, then go to Miles Cross and wait there, because the Faery Queen with all her knights and courtiers will ride past on the stroke of midnight, on her way to dance on the green grass of Carterhaugh."

"But how shall I know you among so many valiant knights and brave courtiers?" fair Janet asked.

"Listen to me carefully, Janet," Tamlane said, "because then my fate will be in your hands, and though Faeryland is indeed beautiful, my heart longs to be with you and with my own kind again.

"When you stand by the cross on Hallowe'en, first you will hear the sound of faery pipes and the beating of faery drums, and a standard bearer carrying a red banner will lead past the first company; but do not stir or move a muscle, for I shall not be among them.

"And then a standard bearer carrying a green banner will lead past the second company, but do not stir or move a muscle, for I shall not be among them.

"But when the standard bearer carrying a white banner leads past the third company, then look for me, Janet. The first knight will wear black armour and be mounted on a steed as black as midnight, but he will

not be Tamlane. And the armour of the second knight will be as brown as a chestnut to match the colour of his steed, but he will not be Tamlane. But the third knight will be clad in white and will be riding a milk-white steed, and he will be your Tamlane, Janet.

"I shall wear a gold star on my forehead and a glove on my right hand, but my left hand will be bare. As soon as you see me, seize the bridle reins and pull me from my horse, and then, Janet, then hold me fast no matter what happens, for the Faery Queen will be bitterly angry and will use every trick she knows to make you let me go, and if once you do, I shall be lost to you for ever."

"I shall do as you say and break the spell that binds you to the Faery Queen," fair Janet promised, and she went back to her home, and never during the summer or the autumn did she return to Carterhaugh.

When the last night of October came, Janet wrapped herself in her grass green cloak and set out in the moonlight for Miles Cross. With an anxious heart she waited, and presently she heard the sound of faery pipes and the beating of faery drums and she knew that the procession was on its way past the cross to dance on the green at Carterhaugh.

50

First came the standard bearer carrying the red banner, but Janet hid behind the cross and let his company pass because Tamlane was not among them.

And then came the standard bearer with the green banner, and again Janet kept herself hidden because Tamlane was not among that company. But when the standard bearer carrying the white banner approached, then Janet knew the time had come. With fast beating heart she watched as a knight, in black armour, mounted on a steed as black as midnight, rode past, but he was not Tamlane. And she watched as the second knight, in brown armour to match the colour of his steed, rode past, but he was not Tamlane.

But the third knight rode a milk-white steed: his armour was white and he wore a gold star on his forehead and a glove on his right hand, but his left hand was bare. And he was Tamlane.

Summoning all her courage, Janet ran forward; seizing the bridle of the milk-white horse, she pulled Tamlane off its back and held him in her arms. Immediately the faeries cried out in alarm and anger, and the Queen of the Faeries spurred her horse forward.

"So you think you can escape!" she cried furiously, and lifting one finger of her right hand, she changed Tamlane into a green lizard that quivered and wriggled and struggled to be free. But Janet looked into the creature's soft grey eyes, and held it fast and would not let it go.

Darker grew the face of the Faery Queen; now she lifted up her right hand, and immediately Tamlane was changed into a green snake which curved and writhed and struggled to be free. But Janet gazed into its sorrowful eyes, and held it fast and would not let it go.

"So you would match yourself against the Queen of the Faeries!" the Queen cried, lifting her right arm, and now Tamlane was a wild deer, kicking and fighting and struggling to be free. But Janet gazed into its imploring eyes, and held it fast and would not let it go.

And the Queen of the Faeries realized that now, at last, Janet had broken the spell and that there was nothing she could do to keep Tamlane in her service. Slowly she raised her left hand and changed Tamlane into his mortal shape. At once fair Janet threw her green cloak over him and together they stood by the cross and watched as the faery procession, with the Queen in its midst, rode on to Carterhaugh.

The next day, which was Hallo'day, fair Janet and Tamlane plighted their troth, and on Ne'erday, which is the first day of the New Year, the bells of the steeple of Selkirk Church pealed joyously to announce to all the good people who dwelt by Yarrow and Ettrick Water that Tamlane, son of the Earl of Murray, who had once been bewitched by the Queen of the Faeries, had just wed the fair Lady Janet, whose love and whose courage had broken the spell and set him free.

The Boy of the Red Twilight Sky

Long ago there dwelt on the shores of the Great Water in the West a young man and his younger wife. They had no children and they lived all by themselves far from other people on an island not far from the coast.

The man spent his time in catching the deep-sea fish far out on the ocean, or in spearing salmon in the distant rivers. Often he was gone for many days and his wife was very lonely in his absence. She was not afraid, for she had a stout spirit, but it was very dismal in the evenings to look only at the grey leaden sky and to hear only the sound of the surf as it beat upon the beach. So day after day she said to herself, "I wish we had children. They would be good company for me when I am alone and my husband is far away."

One evening at twilight when she was solitary because of her husband's absence on the ocean

catching the deep-sea fish, she sat on the sand beach looking out across the water. The sky in the west was pale grey; it was always dull and grey in that country, and when the sun had gone down there was no soft light. In her loneliness the woman said to herself, "I wish we had children to keep me company."

A Kingfisher, with his children, was diving for minnows not far away. And the woman said, "Oh, sea bird with the white collar, I wish we had children like you." And the Kingfisher said, "Look in the sea-shells; look in the sea-shells," and flew away.

The next evening the woman sat again upon the beach looking westward at the dull grey sky. Not far away a white Sea-gull was riding on the waves in the midst of her brood of little ones. And the woman said, "Oh, white sea bird, I wish we had children like you to keep us company." And the Sea-gull said, "Look in the sea-shells; look in the sea-shells," and flew away.

The woman wondered greatly at the words of the Kingfisher and the Sea-gull. As she sat there in thought she heard a strange cry coming from the sand dunes behind her. She went closer to the sound and found that the cry came from a large sea-shell lying on the sand. She picked up the shell, and inside of it was a tiny boy, crying as hard as he could.

She was well pleased with her discovery, and she carried the baby to her home and cared for him. When her husband came home from the sea, he, too, was very happy to find the baby there, for he knew that they would be lonely no more.

The baby grew very rapidly, and soon he was able to walk and move about where he pleased. One day the woman was wearing a copper bracelet on her arm and the child said to her, "I must have a bow made from the copper on your arm." So to please him she made him a tiny bow from the bracelet, and two tiny arrows. At once he set out to hunt game, and day after day he came home bearing the products of his chase. He brought home geese and ducks and brant and small sea birds, and gave them to his mother for food.

As he grew older, the man and his wife noticed that his face took on a golden hue brighter than the colour of his copper bow. Wherever he went there was a strange light. When he sat on the beach looking to the west the weather was always calm and there were strange bright gleams upon the water. And his foster-parents wondered greatly at this unusual power. But the boy would not talk about it; when they spoke of it he was always silent.

It happened once that the winds blew hard over the Great Water and the man could not go out to catch fish because of the turbulent sea. For many days he stayed on shore, for the ocean, which was usually at peace, was lashed into a great fury and the waves were dashing high on the beach. Soon the people were in need of fish for food. And the boy said, "I will go out

with you, for I can overcome the Storm Spirit." The man did not want to go, but at last he listened to the boy's entreaties and together they set out for the fishing grounds far across the tossing sea.

They had not gone far when they met the Spirit of the Storm coming madly from the south-west, where the great winds dwelt. He tried hard to upset their boat, but over them he had no power, for the boy guided the frail craft across the water and all around them the sea was calm and still. Then the Storm Spirit called his nephew Black Cloud to help him, and away in the south-east they saw him hurrying to his uncle's aid. But the boy said to the man, "Be not afraid, for I am more than a match for him." So the two met, but when Black Cloud saw the boy he quickly disappeared. Then the Spirit of the Storm called Mist of the Sea to come and cover the water, for he thought the boat would be lost if he hid the land from the man and the boy. When the man saw Mist of the Sea coming like a grey vapour across the water he was very frightened, for of all his enemies on the ocean he feared this one most. But the boy said, "He cannot harm you when I am with you." And sure enough, when Mist of the Sea saw the boy sitting smiling in the boat he disappeared as quickly as he had come. And the Storm Spirit in great anger hurried away to other parts, and that day there was no more danger on the sea near the fishing grounds.

The boy and the man soon reached the fishing grounds in safety. And the boy taught his foster-father a magic song with which he was able to lure fish to his nets. Before evening came the boat was filled with good fat fish and they set out for their home. The man said, "Tell me the secret of your power." But the boy said, "It is not yet time."

The next day the boy killed many birds. He skinned them all and dried their skins. Then he dressed himself in the skin of a plover and rose into the air and flew above the sea. And the sea under him was grey like his wings. Then he came down and dressed himself in the skin of a blue-jay and soared away again. And the sea over which he was flying was at once changed to blue like the blue of his wings. When he came back to the beach, he put on the skin of a robin with the breast of a golden hue like his face. Then he flew high and at once the waves under him reflected a colour as of fire and bright gleams of light appeared upon the ocean, and the sky in the west was golden red.

The boy flew back to the beach and he said to his foster-parents, "Now it is time for me to leave you. I am the offspring of the sun. Yesterday my power was tested and it was not found wanting, so now I must go away and I shall see you no more. But at evening I shall appear to you often in the twilight sky in the west. And when the sky and the sea look at evening like the colour of my face, you will know that there will be no wind nor storm and that on the morrow the weather will be fair. But although I go away, I shall leave you a strange power. And always when you need me, let me know your desires by making white offerings to me, so that I may see them from my home far in the west."

Then he gave to his foster-mother a wonderful robe. He bade his parents good-bye, and soared away to the west, leaving them in sadness. But the woman still keeps a part of the power he gave her, and when she sits on the island in a crevice in the dunes and loosens her wonderful robe, the wind hurries down from the land, and the sea is ruffled with storm; and the more she loosens the garment the greater is the tempest. But in the late autumn when the cold mists come in from the sea, and the evenings are chill, and the sky is dull and grey, she remembers the promise of the boy. And she makes to him an offering of tiny white feathers plucked from the breasts of birds. She throws them into the air, and they appear as flakes of snow and rise thickly into the winds. And they hurry westward to tell the boy that the world is grey and dreary as it yearns for the sight of his golden face.

Then he appears to the people of earth. He comes at evening and lingers after the sun has gone, until the twilight sky is red, and the ocean in the west has gleams of golden light. And the people then know that there will be no wind and that on the morrow the weather will be fair, as he promised them long ago.

THE PEOPLE COULD FLY

They say the people could fly. Say that long ago in Africa, some of the people knew magic. And they would walk up on the air like climbin' up on a gate. And they flew like blackbirds over the fields. Black, shiny wings flappin' against the blue up there.

Then, many of the people were captured for slavery. The ones that could fly shed their wings. They couldn't take their wings across the water on the slave ships. Too crowded, don't you know.

The folks were full of misery, then. Got sick with the up and down of the sea. So they forgot about

63

flyin' when they could no longer breathe the sweet scent of Africa.

Say the people who could fly kept their power, although they shed their wings. They kept their secret magic in the land of slavery. They looked the same as the other people from Africa who had been comin' over, who had dark skin. Say you couldn't tell any more one who could fly from one who couldn't.

One such who could was an old man, call him Toby. And standin' tall, yet afraid, was a young woman who once had wings. Call her Sarah. Now Sarah carried a babe tied to her back. She trembled to be so hard worked and scorned.

The slaves laboured in the fields from sun-up to sun-down. The owner of the slaves callin' himself their Master. Say he was a hard lump of clay. A hard, glinty coal. A hard rock pile, wouldn't be moved. His Overseer on horseback pointed out the slaves who were slowin' down. So the one called Driver cracked his whip over the slow ones to make them move faster. That whip was a slice-open cut of pain. So they did move faster. Had to.

Sarah hoed and chopped the row as the babe on her back slept.

Say the child grew hungry. That babe started up bawlin' too loud. Sarah couldn't stop to feed it. Couldn't stop to soothe it and quiet it down. She let it cry. She didn't want to. She had no heart to croon to it.

"Keep that thing quiet," called the Overseer. He pointed his finger at the babe. The woman scrunched low. The Driver cracked his whip across the babe anyhow. The babe hollered like any hurt child, and the woman fell to the earth.

The old man was there, Toby, came and helped her to her feet.

"I must go soon," she told him.

"Soon," he said.

Sarah couldn't stand up straight any longer. She was too weak. The sun burned her face. The babe cried and cried, "Pity me, oh, pity me," say it sounded like. Sarah was so sad and starvin', she sat down in the row.

"Get up, you black cow," called the Overseer. He pointed his hand, and the Driver's whip snarled round Sarah's legs. Her sack dress tore into rags. Her legs bled on to the earth. She couldn't get up.

Toby was there where there was no one to help her and the babe.

"Now, before it's too late," panted Sarah. "Now, Father!"

"Yes, Daughter, the time is come," Toby answered. "Go, as you know how to go!"

He raised his arms, holding them out to her: *"Kum ... yali, kum buba tambe,"* and more magic words, said so quickly, they sounded like whispers and sighs.

The young woman lifted one foot on the air. Then the other. She flew clumsily at first, with the child now held tightly in her arms. Then she felt the magic, the African mystery. Say she rose just as free as a bird. As light as a feather.

The Overseer rode after her, hollerin'. Sarah flew over the fences. She flew over the woods. Tall trees could not snag her. Nor could the Overseer. She flew like an eagle now, until she was gone from sight. No one dared speak about it. Couldn't believe it. But it was, because they that was there saw that it was.

Say the next day was dead hot in the fields. A young man slave fell from the heat. The Driver come and whipped him. Toby come over and spoke words to the fallen one. The words of ancient Africa once heard are never remembered completely. The young man forgot them as soon as he heard them. They went way inside him. He got up and rolled over on the air. He rode it awhile. And he flew away.

Another and another fell from the heat. Toby was there. He cried out to the fallen and reached his arms out to them: *"Kum kunka yali, kum ... tambe!"* Whispers and sighs. And they too rose on the air. They rode the hot breezes. The ones flyin' were black and shinin' sticks, wheelin' above the head of the Overseer.

66

They crossed the rows, the fields, the fences, the streams, and were away.

"Seize the old man!" cried the Overseer. "I heard him say the magic *words*. Seize him!"

The one callin' himself Master come runnin'. The Driver got his whip ready to curl round old Toby and tie him up. The slave owner took his hip gun from its place. He meant to kill old, black Toby.

But Toby just laughed. Say he threw back his head and said, "Hee, hee! Don't you know who I am? Don't you know some of us in this field?" He said it to their faces. "We are the ones who fly!"

And he sighed the ancient words that were a dark promise. He said them all around to the others in the field under the whip: *"... buba yali ... buba tambe ..."*

There was a great outcryin'. The bent backs straighted up. Old and young who were called slaves and could fly joined hands. Say like they would ring-sing. But they didn't shuffle in a circle. They didn't sing. They rose on the air. They flew in a flock that was black against the heavenly blue. Black crows or black shadows. It didn't matter, they went so high. Way above the plantation, way over the slavery land. Say they flew away to *Freedom*.

And the old man, old Toby, flew behind them, takin' care of them. He wasn't cryin'. He wasn't laughin'. He was the seer. His gaze fell on the plantation where the slaves who could not fly waited.

Take us with you! Their looks spoke it but they were afraid to shout it. Toby couldn't take them with him. Hadn't the time to teach them to fly. They must wait for a chance to run.

"Goodie-bye!" The old man called Toby spoke to them, poor souls! And he was flyin' gone.

So they say. The Overseer told it. The one called Master said it was a lie, a trick of the light. The Driver kept his mouth shut.

The slaves who could not fly told about the people who could fly to their children. When they were free. When they sat close before the fire in the free land, they told it. They did so love firelight and *Freedom* and tellin'.

They say that the children of the ones who could not fly told their children. And now, me, I have told it to you.

THE BLACK BULL
OF NORROWAY

A poor washerwoman had three daughters, and nothing to give them but her skill in washing clothes. One day the eldest daughter said, "Mother, bake me buns and boil me beef, for I'm going to seek my fortune." She took the food in the basket, walked all night and walked all day, and at evening came to the house of a witch and her daughter beside the wood.

"If it's your fortune you're seeking," said the witch, "stay here by the window and watch. You'll know it when it comes."

The girl gazed out of the window all the first day and all the second day, and saw nothing. On the third day a carriage drew up at the gate, with a coachman, four prancing horses and two liveried footmen.

"My fortune's here. Goodbye!" shouted the girl, and drove off in the carriage while the witch's daughter watched from the shadows with envy in her eyes.

The washerwoman's first daughter was never seen in those parts again.

Some time after she disappeared, the second daughter said, "Mother, cut me cake and slice me sausage, for I'm going to seek my fortune."

She walked all night and walked all day, and at evening came to the same witch's house beside the wood. For three days, as the witch instructed her, she gazed out of the window and saw nothing, but on the fourth day a carriage drew up at the gate, with a coachman, six prancing horses and four liveried footmen, and she drove away while the witch's daughter watched from the shadows with envy in her eyes.

The washerwoman's second daughter was never seen in those parts again.

Soon after she disappeared, the youngest daughter, Meg, said, "Mother, please butter me bread and choose me cheese, for I'm going to seek my fortune."

She went to the witch's house beside the wood, and for a week of days looked out, as the witch instructed her, and saw nothing. Then, on the first day of the second week, the Black Bull of Norroway lumbered down the road, and the witch said, "There you are. You came to seek your fortune, and there it is." She bundled terrified Meg on the bull's broad back, and she and her daughter watched them leave with malice in their eyes.

The bull carried Meg all day, all night, until they came in sight of a grey-green castle in a river valley.

"This is my first brother's house," he said, "and it's here we must stay tonight."

The people of the castle helped Meg from the bull's back, turned the bull loose into a cloverfield, and gave her a magnificent banquet and a goose-feather bed to pass the night. Next morning, as she was climbing on the bull's back ready to ride, they gave her a grey-green apple, sweet scented and unblemished, and said, "Don't cut it till you're in the first great need of your life."

The bull carried Meg all day, all night, all day, to a yellow castle beside a stream.

"This is my second brother's house," he said, "and it's here we must stay tonight."

The people of the castle entertained Meg exactly as before, and in the morning gave her a sweet-scented, unblemished pear and told her not to cut it till she was in the second great need of her life.

The third castle was purple velvet, and this time Meg's gift was a sweet-scented, unblemished plum and her advice was to save it until she was in the third great need of her life.

Soon after they left the third castle, Meg and the bull passed into a dark valley overhung with cliffs, and there was no daylight.

The bull set Meg down by a rock and said, "Wait here. Unless I fight and kill the Guardian of Glass Valley, we'll never get out of here alive. Sit on this rock, and if everything turns blue and sunny, you'll know I've won. If everything turns blood-red, you'll know I've lost. Above all, don't move. If you alter your position by a hair, I'll never be able to find you here again."

Meg sat on the rock and waited. After a while the sun began to shine in a blue sky, the cliffs round her and the ground underfoot turned blue, and she knew that the bull had won his fight. She was so overjoyed that she lifted one foot and crossed it over the other, and the result was that when the bull lumbered back up the valley, his black coat spotted with blood from the battle, though she could see him perfectly, he neither noticed her sitting there nor heard her cries, and never saw or spoke to her again.

Heartbroken, Meg got up to walk on her way. At once her feet began slipping and sliding, and she found that the rock underfoot and the rock walls behind her had turned to mirror-smooth, ice-slippery glass. The Guardian of Glass Valley might be dead, but the Valley still remained, and she was trapped like a spider in a bowl: the more she scrambled up the sides, the more she slithered back, bleeding and exhausted. At last there was nothing for it but to crawl on hands and knees round the edge of Glass Valley, looking for a way out.

For days she found nothing and saw no one, and she

wondered if this was the first great need of her life, and if it was time to cut open the apple the bull's first brother had given her. But before she had need of that, she came to a blacksmith's forge on the valley floor, with the glass walls rearing like a glacier behind it, and sobbed out her story.

"Is that all?" said the smith. "Work for me seven years without complaining, pumping the bellows and holding the tongs, and I'll make a pair of iron shoes to help you out."

For seven years Meg pumped the bellows and held the tongs, and though her brain swam and her cheeks baked in the heat of the furnace, she never once complained.

At the end of the seven years the smith made her a pair of iron shoes set with spikes, and since he knew no other way of fastening them, nailed them to her feet. She clambered and groped her way up the smooth sides of Glass Valley, and every step meant agony. At last she climbed over the rim, staggered out and crawled back to the cottage of the witch and her daughter and begged for shelter.

"It's a good thing you're here," said the witch. "Last night the Prince of Norroway left a suit of clothes for cleaning, black leather spotted and stained with blood, and whoever can clean them is to be his wife. I've tried and my daughter's tried, and the stains sink in ever deeper. You're a washerwoman's daughter: you can earn your keep by cleaning them."

Meg dragged herself to the cleaning stones on her rags of feet, laid the leather clothes flat and began rubbing them with a wash-leather, as her mother had taught her long ago, to clean off the blood.

As soon as the wash-leather touched them the blood stains vanished, the leather shone, and Meg's feet healed as if they'd never known a moment's injury.

She ran back to the cottage with the clothes over her arm, and the witch snatched them and cackled, "Thank you, my dear. You've made my daughter's fortune," and locked her in the attic in case she saw the Prince of Norroway or spoke to him.

That night the prince came to fetch his clothes, the witch's daughter smiled a gap-toothed smile and told him she'd scrubbed and struggled to get them clean, and he had no choice but to agree to marry her in three days' time.

That night, alone in the attic, Meg remembered the apple she'd been given in the first brother's castle of the Black Bull of Norroway. This was certainly the first great need of her life. She cut the apple in two, and instead of pips, it was filled with pearls. She called to the witch's daughter and said, "Let me sing outside the prince's door tonight, and these pearls are yours."

"Done!" said the daughter. But she ran straight to her mother, and her mother gave the prince a sleeping potion in a wine cup.

That night, Meg sat outside his door and sang:

Seven years I served for thee;
Glass Hill I climbed for thee;
Thy clothes I washed for thee;
Wake up and turn to me.

But the sleeping potion clogged his ears so that he heard not a single word, and by the time he called for his breakfast next morning, Meg was locked in her attic again and nowhere to be seen.

It was the second great need of her life, and she sliced open the pear she'd been given in the second brother's castle of the Black Bull of Norroway. Its core was of twisted gold. She called to the witch's daughter and said, "Let me sing another night outside the prince's door, and this gold is yours."

"Done!" said the daughter. But once again she ran straight to her mother, and once again the witch gave the prince a sleeping potion in a wine cup.

All night long Meg sat outside his door and sang:

Seven years I served for thee;
Glass Hill I climbed for thee;
Thy clothes I washed for thee;
Wake up and turn to me.

But the sleeping potion clogged his ears as before, and by the time he called for his breakfast next morning, Meg was locked up in her attic and nowhere to be seen.

It was the third great need of her life, and when she cut open the plum she found instead of a stone a diamond quarried from Glass Valley, as big as a pigeon's egg. "Let me sing one last night outside the prince's door," she said to the witch's daughter, "and take this stone for your wedding crown."

"Done!" said the witch's daughter, and her mother prepared a sleeping potion as before.

But just as the prince was lifting it to his lips, he heard a faint lowing of cattle from the meadow outside his window, as if the bull's three brothers were calling him, got up to look, knocked the wine cup over and spilled the wine. He went to bed, thinking nothing of it, and had hardly slept five minutes when he heard Meg singing outside his door:

Seven years I served for thee;
Glass Hill I climbed for thee;
Thy clothes I washed for thee;
Wake up and turn to me.

The prince ran and opened the door, and Meg fell into her true lover's arms. They were married next morning, and every bell in Norroway pealed in celebration. As for the witch and her daughter, they sat down to comfort themselves by counting out the pearls, gold and diamond they had cheated out of Meg, and found nothing in their hands but apple pips, a pear core and a plum stone. Shrieking with rage, they galloped like maddened cattle to the edge of the meadow, tumbled over the rim of Glass Valley and never troubled the mortal world again.

MIRRAGEN
THE CAT-MAN

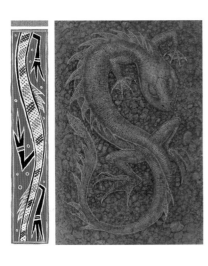

In New South Wales two mighty rivers flow together, and at their junction is a deep, clear water hole, which was once the home of the monster Gurangatch. Descended from a long line of ancestors, some of whom were lizards and some fish, Gurangatch was half-lizard, half-fish.

He had grown to an enormous size, but the deep hole at the confluence of the rivers was large enough to accommodate him and give him freedom to move about. On account of his size he was never molested by fish or birds, nor even by man until one day Mirragen the Cat-man came that way.

Mirragen the Cat-man was the most famous fisherman in all that part of Australia. With net and spear he could seek out the wiliest fish and entangle it in the meshes, or impale it on his many-pronged spear.

He did not rely on skill alone, but had also a knowledge of spells which would lure the fish from their hiding places and draw them within reach of his spear. He was a traveller, too, always seeking fresh experiences, and priding himself on the many different kinds of fish he had caught and eaten. Little fish he despised. Only the biggest were considered fair game by Mirragen, and if they were large enough to provide sport as well as food, he was well content.

For a long time now he had had to satisfy himself with smaller fish from the rivers and lakes which were his usual hunting grounds, and he had become discontented.

"Remain here," he had said to his family. "You are safe in this valley, and there are plenty of roots and small game in the hills to keep hunger at bay. I am going away for a time. When I return I will bring back the biggest fish you have ever seen."

They tried to dissuade him, but he was adamant.

"Eels!" he exclaimed scornfully, when they pointed out that the river by their camp was full of fat eels. "They are lazy and easy to catch, and there is not a single one as long as my arm. They are food for babies. I am off to find a fish that is worthy of a man's skill."

When he came to the junction of the two rivers his eyes lit up and his stride lengthened.

"The very place I am looking for!" he exclaimed.

Placing his dilly bag and fishing gear on the ground, he crawled forward on hands and knees and put his head over the edge of a cliff where he could look straight down into the water hole. At first he could see nothing but green water, but as his eyes grew accustomed to the gloom at the foot of the cliff, his gaze went deeper and deeper into the water, as though he were actually swimming through it. Further down he went, and suddenly he found that he was looking into two enormous, unblinking eyes.

"Gurangatch!"

The name came naturally to him, for he had heard vague rumours of an enormous reptile or fish that lived at the bottom of a deep pool where two rivers flowed together.

He repeated the most powerful spells he had learned from the Wirinuns, and slowly Gurangatch floated towards the surface, struggling in vain against the unseen power that was drawing him upwards. The sweat ran down Mirragen's face and dropped into the water, but in spite of the magic power that was being exerted, he was unable to hold the monster,

83

which drifted down once more into the safety of the water hole.

"Tomorrow!" Mirragen thought; and he sharpened the prongs of his spear before lying down to sleep. "Tomorrow he will not escape me, even if I have to dive into the pool to transfix him with my spear. This is indeed the prize that I promised to bring home to my tribe. If I succeed, I shall be remembered for ever as the killer of Gurangatch."

⊠　⊠　⊠

The monster was really frightened. For many years he had lived in the pool, confident that no one could harm him because of his size, and he had not been prepared for Mirragen's magic. He knew that when the sun rose the Cat-man would be waiting for him, armed with more than magic.

Sure enough, when the sun's first rays lit the top of the cliff, Mirragen's spear flashed down and rang against his scales, but they were hard enough to turn the prongs. He waited for the next move, knowing that Mirragen's net would be equally useless, but dreading some new device that he would be powerless to resist.

Presently Gurangatch began to feel sleepy. It did not seem to matter any longer what Mirragen did, and his mind began to drift away on a tide of unconsciousness.

He was brought back to life with a shock when he felt himself begin to float upwards. There was a strange taste in his mouth, and he knew that the Cat-man had poisoned the water with a tincture of bark. It was not sufficient to kill him, but enough to sharpen his senses and make him aware of the danger that was threatening him.

"I must get away from the pool before he catches me in the clutch of his magic powers," he thought.

With a flick of his powerful tail he turned round and began to burrow into the solid rock. Leaving the home of his ancestors behind him, he swam through the ground almost as easily as if it were water. Earth, rocks and sand were ploughed up in an immense wave, and as he wriggled through the new element, the river turned in its course and filled the channel with a foaming torrent of water.

⊠   ⊠   ⊠

Mirragen was not aware that Gurangatch had left, for he was hunting for more poisonous bark. When he returned he rubbed his eyes. A third mighty river was now flowing through the land, dwindling to a thread of silver in the distance. Picking up his net and spears, he ran along the bank. Tiny landslides kept slipping into the river and he had to watch his step lest he should slide down with them and be carried away in the flood.

As the heat of the day was ebbing, he reached the end of the stream. It had changed course several times when Gurangatch had met with a solid outcrop of rock, but at last it had come to an end, and plunged underground. Mirragen debated whether he should follow it into the

cave where it disappeared, but he knew that he was no match for a monster in the dark chasms of the earth. He climbed a small hill above the cave and dug down into the soil until he felt it give way beneath him. Tying several of his fish spears together, he probed the hole, hoping that the monster might be somewhere beneath. Failing in this, he dug another, and another, but succeeded only in piercing the rock with deep holes which remain to this day above the Whambeyan caves to witness to his attempts to reach Gurangatch.

But the monster had felt the spear slithering past his flanks, and realized that if he stayed there he must fall victim to this relentless fisherman. Once again he dug through the ground, and as he twisted and turned he came out into the valley where Mirragen had left his family. They saw him coming.

First the mighty head broke the side of the valley, then the great body slithered down the side almost to their feet, and along the furrow the water raced in a torrent like a tidal wave confined to a narrow bed. The water foamed over the edges and splashed against the rocks, licking at the heels of the women and children as they raced for safety up the far side of the valley.

There they met a weary man who had been travelling along the crest of the ridges.

"Mirragen, husband," cried his wives, "stay with us! We are afraid. The monster is devastating the land and we have barely escaped with our lives. Even if you were

to catch up with him you could not overcome such a monster. Be satisfied with the eels in our little stream and remain with us."

"There will be no eels here now, nor any little stream," laughed Mirragen. "The stream is a great river now, but it will be a long time before fish come into these waters. If I do not catch Gurangatch now I will never rest content. This is my destiny."

He ran on and on, and by nightfall he had caught up with the lizard-fish. Mirragen's body and limbs were torn by sharp rocks and he was faint through loss of blood. He plunged his spear into the monster's side, but again the spear points glanced off the scales, and Gurangatch's tail swung round and knocked Mirragen off his feet. In the gathering darkness they fought, until the rocks were worn smooth. Gurangatch slid off them and resumed his journey, but Mirragen was now too tired and bruised to follow.

Morning came and he took up the chase again.

"Gurangatch is getting weary, but so am I," he thought. "If we fight again I may get the worst of it. The time has come to get help."

He turned back and went to a camp where he knew he would find some of his tribe. They were sitting down to their evening meal when he arrived, and greeted him enthusiastically.

"Welcome, Mirragen," they cried. "Have you brought some new fish for us to eat?"

The Cat-man sank down with a groan.

"I am weary and hurt," he said. "For day after day I

have been following Gurangatch, and I have nearly caught him."

They opened their eyes wide. "Gurangatch? No one could ever hope to catch Gurangatch!"

"Well, I have!" Mirragen snapped. "I cast magic spells over him. I poisoned the water where he lived and drove him out. I have been chasing him through valleys and over hills, and under the earth. He is at the point of death, and all that remains is to put an end to his sufferings. I am a generous man, so I invite you to help me and share the honour that will come to me."

"Not us!" they said promptly. "You don't look very fit, Mirragen. It looks as though you have been in a fight

89

and have had the worst of it. We would rather stay here and eat the delicious eels we caught this morning."

Mirragen got up with an exclamation of disgust. "I will find someone else to share the glory," he said.

"You might try the Bird-men further down the valley," one of his relatives suggested.

As he stumbled off into the night, Mirragen thought that this might be a good idea, especially if some of them were diving birds, for he suspected that Gurangatch had taken refuge in a water hole, and he was too tired to begin the whole sequence over again.

The Shags and Divers and Ducks were ready to help him, and they travelled with him along the trail that was so clearly marked by the newly formed rivers, until in the morning they came to a large pool where the river ended, disappearing into the ground where Gurangatch in his struggles had formed the underground mazes of the Jenolan caves.

One of the Ducks paddled across the hole, bobbed his tail in the air, and sank down into the water. They waited a long time for him to return, but when he appeared he swam quickly to the bank, waddled ashore and began to walk back towards his home.

"What have you seen?" shouted Mirragen.

Duck flicked his tail and said shortly, "The hole is bottomless. There's nothing there."

Shag was the next to try. He fluttered over the water, closed his wings, and plummeted down into the depths. He came up with a small fish in his beak, which he brought ashore and laid at Mirragen's feet.

"Is this Gurangatch?" he asked.

The Cat-man was so exasperated that he kicked it back into the pool, and Shag fled in case Mirragen should do him an injury.

Only Diver Bird was left.

"Please try," Mirragen begged. "The others were afraid, but I know you will help me."

Diver flew high up into the air and fell towards the pool like a flash of lightning. The water closed over him. He was gone so long that Mirragen began to fear for the life of his friend, but at last he bobbed up and swam ashore.

"Gurangatch is there," Diver said, "but you will never catch him. All I could do was to bring you a little part of the monster that I could carry in my beak."

He gave a piece of flesh to his friend. It was covered with large silver scales that twinkled in the sunlight.

The Cat-man put his arm round the bird. "You are my friend," he said. "It is the end of the chase. Let Gurangatch lie there for ever. We have his flesh and we will eat it together to show him that we are the victors."

The flesh was soon eaten, but the Whambeyan and Jenolan caves, and many rivers of New South Wales, remain to show how Mirragen the Cat-man chased Gurangatch the monster in the Dreamtime and ate a piece of him as a token of victory.

The Girl Who Couldn't Walk

Once there was a girl who couldn't walk. Every day her father would carry her downstairs and put her in a chair by the window, and she would sit watching children playing in the lane on their way to school, running and skipping, chasing one another.

She loved to watch them. She was a happy child because it was her nature to be happy. She had never known what it would be like to walk, so she never complained. But her parents were not happy. Her mother complained all the time because she had been cursed with a child who could not walk. She wanted her daughter to be like all the other children. And her father complained because he had to carry her up and down stairs every day.

They brought doctors from all over the country to see what they could do for her, and the doctors would spend a long time examining her, and some would give her potions and some would give her exercises, some would stretch her and some would bend her, and they all ended up telling her parents the same thing: "I'm sorry, but your daughter will never walk."

"Send for another doctor," her mother would say. "Surely somebody can help her."

The girl would gaze out of her window and watch everything that was going on outside. She would wave to the children running down the lane, and she would watch the birds flying and the flowers unfolding and the clouds racing across the sky. She saw everything that was happening in the world outside her house, right up to the top slopes of the hill where the wild hares played. That was what she loved to look at most.

One day she noticed an old woman coming down the hill to the lane. The old woman was so bent that she had to use a stick, and her feet shuffled slowly along. It took her so long to come down the lane that the sun had moved from one side of the house to the other before she reached the gate, but the girl never took her eyes off her the whole time.

The old woman shuffled down the path and at last reached the front door. She came into the room and stood in front of the girl, gazing at her and nodding her head, and then she turned to the parents.

"I can give her what she most wants," she told them.

"You!" scorned the girl's mother. "How can you cure her?"

"The best doctors in the world have tried, and all failed. What can you do?" the girl's father asked.

"Magic," said the old woman. "Magic."

The parents both turned their backs on her at once.

"You can each have one wish," the old woman said, "but you must keep it in your hearts. Once a wish is spoken the wish is broken. Remember that." And with that she went out of the house.

"What a stupid old woman," the mother said. "There's only one wish any of us can have, and that is for our daughter to walk. What can she do about that?"

As soon as she spoke there came such a rushing of wind that it seemed as if the whole house might fly up into the air. The doors and windows blew open, the carpets were lifted off the floor, the curtains billowed out like puffs of smoke, and all the cups and plates rattled on the shelves like chattering teeth. And with the wind came a voice, shrieking through the open doors and windows like a great cry of pain.

"You have wasted your wish! You have wasted your wish! A wish spoken is a wish broken!"

The girl's mother clapped her hand to her mouth.

"What have I done!" she cried. "Now she'll never be like other children!" Her husband put his arm round her and comforted her.

They both turned to look at their daughter but she was gazing out of the window at the old woman, who had made her slow way to the end of the lane. She saw the old woman shrinking down. She saw her crouch so she was almost touching the ground with her arms. She saw her hair turning brown and laughed with joy and reached out towards the window, as if for the very first time she wanted to be on the other side of it.

The next day she was watching the hillside and saw what she was looking for. She said nothing to her parents. At last the old woman reached the lane and started her slow journey towards the house, and still the girl said nothing. The door opened, and in the old woman came. She stood in front of the girl, gazing at her and nodding her head, and then she turned to the parents.

"Can you really make our daughter walk?" the girl's mother asked her.

"I told you what I can do," the old woman said.

"And can you really do it by magic?"

"Magic," the old woman nodded. "But you've had your wish. You've wasted it."

"I didn't believe in your magic. I didn't understand! Please can I try again?"

But the old woman turned away from the mother and spoke to her husband. "You still have your wish," she said. "Use it well."

"Can I have the same wish as my wife?" the man asked her.

"No." The old woman shook her head and shuffled out of the house and down the lane.

The man sat with his head in his hands.

"You have your wish!" his wife said. "You can use it to make our daughter better. Use it."

"How can I? There's only one wish I would make, and you've wasted it! What else can I ask for?"

"Say it in a different way!" his wife suggested. Wish that..."

"Ssh!" her husband warned her. "A wish spoken is a wish broken, remember."

"But I'm only making suggestions," his wife said. "I can't have a wish anyway, so what I say doesn't count. Wish that..."

The husband put his hand across his wife's mouth. "Of course it counts! If it's spoken, it's spoken, isn't it! Leave it to me!"

He sat down again turning over in his head different ways of saying the same thing, and at last in despair he burst out, "How I wish you'd kept your mouth shut yesterday!"

As soon as he spoke there came the rushing of the wind, the blowing open of the doors and windows, the lifting up of the carpets and the billowing out of the curtains, and the chattering of crockery on the shelves. And with the wind came a voice, shrieking through the open doors and windows like a great cry of pain.

"You have wasted your wish! You have wasted your wish! A wish spoken is a wish broken!"

But the girl heard nothing of this. She was gazing out of the window at the old woman making her slow way to the end of the lane. She watched her shrink down. She saw her crouch so she was almost touching the ground with her arms. She saw her hair turning brown and growing fast until it covered her body. She saw how her legs grew long and her arms grew short. The girl laughed with joy and reached out towards the window, straining with all her might to be out of the chair and on her feet.

All next day she watched the hillside, and at last she saw what she was looking for. She said nothing to her parents. She watched as the old woman began to walk slowly down the lane, and still she said nothing. She watched her reach the gate and walk up the path to her house. The door opened, and in the old woman came. She stood in front of the girl, gazing at her and nodding her head, and then she turned to the parents.

"I'm sorry," the girl's father said. "I believed in your

magic but I made the wrong wish. Please give me another chance."

"No," said the old woman. "There is no other chance." She turned back to the girl, who was watching every little movement she made. "Now it is your turn to make a wish." And she went out of the house.

Anxiously the girl's mother and father circled round their daughter.

"Don't say a word!" her mother warned her. "You have to think it in your heart. A wish spoken is a wish broken, remember."

"And don't wish what your mother wished for," her father said. "Or it will be a wasted wish."

"I've already made my wish," the girl said.

Instantly there came a rushing of wind such as they had never heard before. The doors and windows blew open and the rugs were lifted off the floor. The curtains billowed out of the windows and all the plates and cups and saucers in the house rattled and chattered and shook. And with the wind came a voice, laughing through the open doors and windows like a great cry of joy.

"She wishes to be like me!"

"Like the old woman!" the girl's mother cried. "What a thing to wish for!"

"What have you done!" her father shouted.

But their daughter heard nothing of this. She was watching the old woman making her slow way up the

lane. She reached out to the window as if she wanted to be on the other side of it. She saw how the old woman shrank, how she crouched to the ground, how her legs grew long and her arms grew short, how her hair turned brown and covered her body. The girl strained out of her chair as if she was trying to stand up. She saw how the old woman's ears grew long, how her eyes grew bright, how she straightened up, how she leapt forward. The girl stepped forward, one pace, two, three ... and with a bound she was away, out of the house, out of the path, out of the lane.

Her parents ran to the window, but all they could see, and all they would ever see, were two brown hares leaping and dancing to the very top of the hill.

THE WOMAN OF THE SEA

One clear summer night, a young man was walking on the sand by the sea on the Isle of Unst. He had been all day in the hayfields and was come down to the shore to cool himself, for it was the full moon and the wind blowing fresh off the water.

As the young man came to the shore he saw the sand shining white in the moonlight and on it the sea-people dancing. He had never seen them before, for they show themselves like seals by day, but on this night because it was midsummer and a full moon, they were dancing for joy. Here and there he saw dark patches where they had flung down their sealskins, but they themselves were as clear as the moon itself, and they cast no shadow.

He crept a little closer, and his own shadow moved before him, and of a sudden one of the sea-people danced upon it. The dance was broken. They looked about and saw him and with a cry they fled to their sealskins and dived into the waves. The air was full of their soft crying and splashing.

But one of the faery people ran hither and thither on the sands wringing her hands as if she had lost something. The young man looked and saw a patch of darkness in his own shadow. It was the seal's skin. Quickly he threw it behind a rock and watched to see what the sea faery would do.

She ran down to the edge of the sea and stood with her feet in the foam, crying to her people to wait for her, but they had gone too far to hear. The moon shone on her and the young man thought she was the loveliest creature he had ever seen. Then she began to weep softly to herself and the sound of it was so pitiful that he could bear it no longer. He stood upright and went down to her.

"What have you lost, woman of the sea?" he asked her.

She turned at the sound of his voice and looked at him, terrified.

For a moment he thought she was going to dive into the sea. Then she came a step nearer and held up her two hands to him.

"Sir," she said, "give it back to me and I and my

people will give you the treasure of the sea." Her voice was like the waves singing in a shell.

"I would rather have you than the treasure of the sea," said the young man. Although she hid her face in her hands and fell again to crying, more hopeless than ever, he was not moved.

"It is my wife you shall be," he said. "Come with me now to the priest, and we will go home to our own house, and it is yourself shall be mistress of all I have. It is warm you will be in the long winter nights, sitting at your own hearth stone and the peat burning red, instead of swimming in the cold green sea."

She tried to tell him of the bottom of the sea where there comes neither snow nor darkness of night and the waves are as warm as a river in summer, but he would not listen. Then he threw his cloak around her and lifted her in his arms and they were married in the priest's house.

He brought her home to his little thatched cottage and into the kitchen with its earthen floor, and set her down before the hearth in the red glow of the peat. She cried out when she saw the fire, for she thought it a strange crimson jewel.

"Have you anything as bonny as that in the sea?" he asked her, kneeling down beside her, and she said, so faintly that he could scarcely hear her, "No."

"I know not what there is in the sea," he said, "but there is nothing on land as bonny as you." For the first time she ceased her crying and sat looking into the heart of the fire. It was the first thing that made her forget, for a moment, the sea which was her home.

All the days she was in the young man's house, she never lost the wonder of the fire and it was the first thing she brought her children to see. For she had three children in the twice seven years she lived with him. She was a good wife to him. She baked his bread and she spun the wool from the fleece of his Shetland sheep.

He never named the seal's skin to her, nor she to him, and he thought she was content, for he loved her dearly and she was happy with her children. Once, when he was ploughing on the headland above the bay, he looked down and saw her standing on the rocks and crying in a mournful voice to a great seal in the water. He said nothing when he came home, for he thought to himself it was not to wonder at if she were lonely for the sight of her own people. As for the seal's skin, he had hidden it well.

There came a September evening and she was busy in the house, and the children playing hide-and-seek in the stacks in the gloaming. She heard them shouting and went out to them.

"What have you found?" she said.

The children came running to her. "It is like a big cat," they said, "but it is softer than a cat. Look!"

She looked and saw her seal's skin that was hidden under last year's hay.

She gazed at it, and for a long time she stood still. It was warm dusk and the air was yellow with the afterglow of the sunset. The children had run away again, and their voices among the stacks sounded like the voices of birds. The hens were on the roost already, and now and then one of them clucked in its sleep. The air was full of little friendly noises from the sleepy talking of the swallows under the thatch. The door was open and the warm smell of the baking of bread came out to her.

She turned to go in, but a small breath of wind rustled over the stacks and she stopped again. It brought a sound that she had heard so long she never seemed to hear it at all. It was the sea whispering down on the sand. Far out on the rocks the great waves broke in a boom, and close in on the sand the little waves slipped racing back. She took up the seal's skin and went swiftly down the track that led to the sands. The children saw her and cried to her to wait for them, but she did not hear them. She was just out of sight when their father came in from the byre and they ran to tell him.

"Which road did she take?" said he.

"The low road to the sea," they answered, but already their father was running to the shore. The children tried to follow him, but their voices died away behind him, so fast did he run.

As he ran across the hard sands, he saw her dive to join the big seal who was waiting for her, and he gave a loud cry to stop her. For a moment she rested on the surface of the sea, then she cried with her voice that was like the waves singing in a shell, "Fare ye well, and all good befall you, for you were a good man to me."

Then she dived to the faery places that lie at the bottom of the sea and the big seal with her.

For a long time her husband watched for her to come back to him and the children; but she came no more.